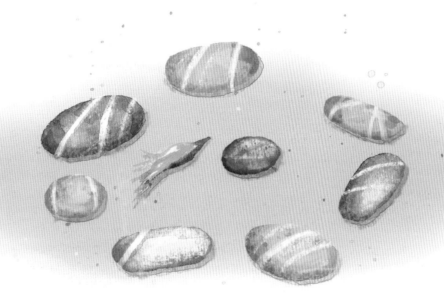

'For Sarah'

Sally Hopgood

D0452913

79 682 084 7

TOP THAT

PUBLISHING LTD

Licensed exclusively to Top That Publishing Ltd
Tide Mill Way, Woodbridge, Suffolk, IP12 1AP, UK
www.topthatpublishing.com
Copyright © 2014 Tide Mill Media
All rights reserved
0 2 4 6 8 9 7 5 3 1
Printed and bound in China

Illustrated by Sam McPhillips
Written by Sally Hopgood

All rights reserved. No part of this publication may be reproduced, stored in
a retrieval system, or transmitted in any form or by any means, electronic,
mechanical, photocopying, recording or otherwise, without the prior written
permission of the publisher. Neither this book nor any part or any of the
illustrations, photographs or reproductions contained in it shall be sold or disposed
of otherwise than as a complete book, and any unauthorised sale of such part
illustration, photograph or reproduction shall be deemed to be a breach of the
publisher's copyright.

ISBN 978-1-78244-538-8

A catalogue record for this book is available from the British Library
Printed and bound in China

Stone Boy and the Girl

Written
by Sally Hopgood

Illustrated
by Sam McPhillips

It was a hot summer's day

and a little girl stood alone on the beach.
The little girl's mean brother had stomped
on her sandcastle and she was trying
desperately hard not to cry.

Sitting by the shore, the little girl was unable to hold back her tears any longer.

As she stared at the ground, they rolled down her face and onto a little round pebble.

Noticing that the pebble looked as if it had a smiling face, the little girl added other pebbles and some seaweed hair to make a boy made entirely of stone.

'Time for tea!' came a distant call and the little girl raced across the sand, leaving the stone boy alone.

As the sun slowly set, the sea crept
slowly up the empty beach and seemed to whisper
to the stone boy ...

'Shhhhhhhhhhhhhhh ...

Shhhhhhhhhhhhhh ...

Shhhhhhhhhhhhhhhhh'

That night, the sky was lit by millions of stars and the sea was glowing too! All of the tiniest ocean creatures had chosen this one special night to rise to the surface and glow as they danced along with the current.

The sea came closer ... and closer ...

until it gently touched the stone boy.

In an instant, Stone Boy's eyes blinked!

'Shhhhhhhhhhhhh,'

whispered the sea.

Slowly, Stone Boy moved his arms ...

then his head ... and his legs!

'shhhhhhhhhhhhhhhh.'

'I am alive!'

he shouted, excitedly.

'Shhhh ...' hushed the sea,
as Stone Boy set off to explore
the beach.

Before long, Stone Boy stumbled across a small plastic bucket, half buried in a mound of sand and stones. It was covered in footprints and lying beside it was a crumpled little paper flag.

'I wonder what happened here?' thought Stone Boy.
'The one who made you built a beautiful castle here,' replied a voice from inside the bucket.
Stone Boy bent down, peered into the bucket and saw a small hermit crab.

'Hello,' said the hermit crab.

'Hello,' replied Stone Boy.

The hermit crab told Stone Boy all about the little girl, the sandcastle and her mean brother.

'She was crying when she made you,' he said.

'I know a way to make her happy!'

cried Stone Boy.

Stone Boy and the hermit crab worked all through the night.
They pushed and patted the sand and collected pretty shells and seaweed from all over the beach.

Before sunrise the next morning,

the little girl woke up.

She drew back the curtains

and couldn't believe her eyes!

There, in the moonlight, stood

the most magnificent sandcastle

that she had ever seen.

And, sitting on top, was a

crumpled little paper flag.

It was too early to get up, so the little girl crept back into bed and waited for morning to come.

After breakfast, the little girl ran to the beach, hoping to see the castle that she had seen last night.

But,
it was gone!

The little girl ran to the place where she had seen the castle from her bedroom window.

'Gone,' she sighed, and dropped her head.

As she stared at the ground, the little girl noticed something familiar in the sand ...

... it was a small pebble with a smiling face.

The girl picked up the pebble and a smile spread across her face.

'It's going to be
a good day today,'

she said, happily.

That evening, the hermit crab spied the little girl's new sandcastle. It was *magnificent!*

'Is Stone Boy coming back?'
he asked the sea.

'Shhhhhhhhhhhhh ...

Shhhhhhhhhhhhhhhh ...

Shhhhhhhhhhhhhhhhh ...'

was all the sea would say.